WORLD OF
DRAGONS
COLORING BOOK

ARKADY ROYTMAN

DOVER PUBLICATIONS, INC.
MINEOLA, NEW YORK

NOTE

In this exciting coloring book, noted artist Arkady Roytman delves into the fascinating world of dragons with thirty action-packed scenes. Experience the power and majesty of these legendary beasts from cultures around the world, including Asia, Europe, and South America. So get your crayons, markers, and colored pencils ready as you meet the Rainbow Serpent from Australia, the deadly Typhon from Ancient Greece, the Niddhog of Norse mythology, and many more fierce monsters! And each illustration comes with an informative caption giving details about dragons.

Bibliographical Note

World of Dragons Coloring Book is a new work, first published by Dover Publications, Inc., in 2014.

International Standard Book Number

ISBN-13: 978-0-486-49445-6
ISBN-10: 0-486-49445-4

Manufactured in the United States by LSC Communications
49445407   2020
www.doverpublications.com

1. Dragon — Dragons are mythical creatures that appear in many different societies and eras. There are two distinct cultural traditions of dragons: European dragons, derived from European folktales and related to Greek and Middle Eastern mythologies, which tend to represent evil, and Chinese dragons, with counterparts in Japan, Korea and other East Asian countries, which tend to be benevolent.

2. Chinese — **Huanglong (Yellow Dragon)** — Chinese dragons are depicted as long, snake-like creatures with four claws (or five for the imperial dragon), and have long been potent symbols of auspicious power in Chinese folklore and art. The Yellow Dragon emerged from the River Luo and presented the legendary Emperor Fu Xi with the elements of writing. Its waking, sleeping, and breathing determined day and night, season and weather.

3. Japanese — **Ryu** — Most Japanese dragons are water deities associated with rainfall and bodies of water, and are typically depicted as large, wingless, serpentine creatures with clawed feet (three claws instead of four). They are considered to be a wise dragon species and can write using Japanese calligraphy. They create ink, use their tails as a brush, and write on shed belly skin. Similar to Chinese dragons, Japanese dragons are usually benevolent and may grant wishes.

4. Vietnamese — **Rong (or Long)** — The dragon is the most important of the four symbolic animals of Vietnamese mythology. According to an ancient origin myth, the Vietnamese people are descended from a dragon and a fairy. Vietnamese dragons are able to control the weather and bring rain. Like the Chinese dragon, the Vietnamese dragon is the symbol of yang, representing the universe, life, existence, and growth.

5. Indian — **Nāga** — In India, dragons are considered nature spirits and the protectors of springs, wells, and rivers. They bring rain, and thus fertility, but are also thought to bring disasters such as floods and drought. They also possess the elixir of life and of immortality. Although they are snakes, some are able to take human form. They tend to be very curious and are only malevolent to humans when they have been mistreated.

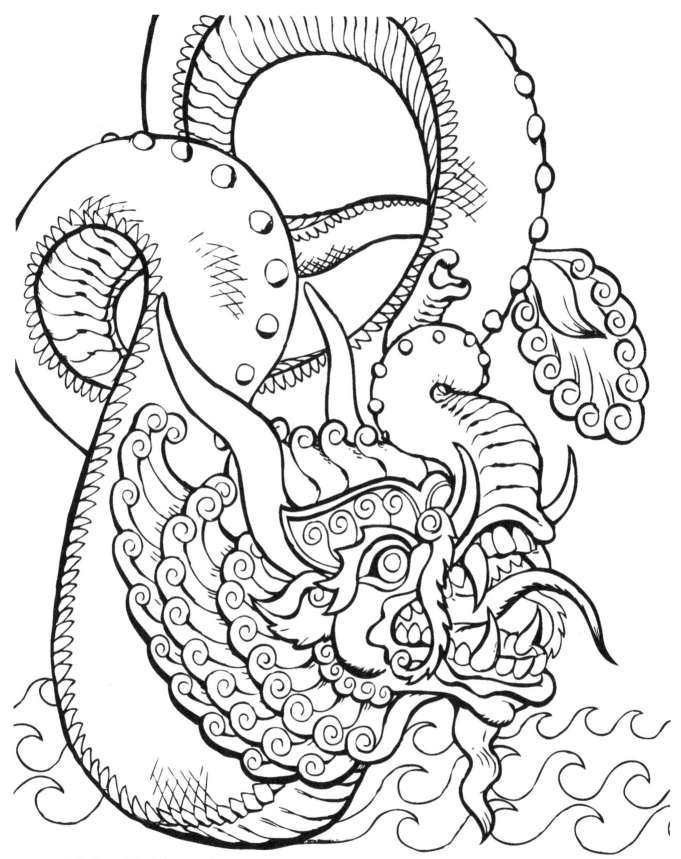

6. Indian (Hindu) — **Makara** — An aquatic mythical creature ("sea dragon" or "water-monster"), the Makara is the vehicle of the Ganga — the goddess of the river Ganges. It has usually been depicted as half animal and half fish, with the forequarters of an elephant and the hindquarters as a fish tail.

7. Khmer — **Neak** — Unlike western dragons, a Khmer dragon has no wings and is benevolent. The Neak is derived from the Indian Nāga. Like its Indian counterpart, the Neak is often depicted with cobra-like characteristics, such as a hood. The number of heads can be as high as nine, with the higher the number the higher the rank of the dragon. Odd-headed dragons symbolize male energy while even headed dragons symbolize female energy.

8. Balinese – **Barong** — A lion-like creature in the mythology of Bali, Indonesia, Barong is the king of the spirits, leader of the forces of good, and the sworn enemy of Rangda, the demon queen. In Balinese culture the fight between Barong and Rangda is acted out as dance to symbolize the eternal battle between good and evil. Barong is usually portrayed as a lion with a red head, covered in white thick fur, and wearing gilded jewelry.

9. Javanese — **Antaboga** — The world serpent of traditional pre-Islamic Javanese mythology, only Antaboga existed at the beginning of time. It meditated and created the world turtle Bedwang from which all other life sprang.

10. Filipino — Bakunawa — A giant sea serpent with a mouth the size of a lake, Bakunawa is said to possess two sets of wings; one large, the other small and found further down its body. It is believed to be the cause of eclipses by rising up from the sea and swallowing the moon whole. To keep it from completely swallowing the moon, ancient Filipinos would go out of their homes with pots and pans and make noise in order to scare the Bakunawa into spitting out the moon back into the sky.

11. Australian — **Rainbow Serpent** — A creator god in the mythology of Australian Aboriginals, the Rainbow Serpent was thought to be the rainbow itself. When it appeared in the sky, it was said that the serpent was moving from one watering hole to another. It is one of the oldest continuing religious beliefs in the world and maintains cultural influence to this day.

12. Greek — **Drakon of Thebes (Ismerian Dragon)** — In Greek mythology dragons commonly had the role of protecting important objects or places. The Drakon of Thebes guarded the famous Ismenian spring of the god Ares. It was eventually slain by the legendary hero Kadmos, who sowed the dragon's teeth in the ground, from which there sprang a race of fierce warriors.

13. Greek — **Lernaean Hydra** — The Hydra was an ancient serpent-like water beast that possessed many heads. Every time a head was cut off it grew two more. Its lair was the lake of Lerna in the Argolid. Beneath the water was an entrance to the Underworld, and the Hydra was its guardian. The Hydra was killed by Heracles as the second of his Twelve Labors.

14. Greek — **Typhon** — The most deadly monster in all of Greek mythology, Typhon was the last son of Gaia, the primordial mother goddess. He was known as the "Father of All Monsters," the largest and most fearsome of the world's creatures. Typhon's human upper half reached as high as the stars, while his hands reached east and west. His bottom half consisted of gigantic hissing vipers. Fire flashed from his eyes, striking fear even into the Gods of Olympus.

15. Hebrew — **Leviathan** — A sea monster referenced in the Old Testament, Leviathan is described by Jewish sources as a dragon who lives over the Source of the Deep and who, along with the land-monster Behemoth, will be given up to the righteous at the end of time. When the Leviathan is hungry, he sends forth from his mouth a heat so intense as to make all the waters of the ocean boil.

16. Mesopotamian (Babylonian) — **Tiamat** — A "Chaos Monster," Tiamat was goddess of the ocean in ancient Mesopotamian religions. She bore many younger gods with her husband Apsu, the god of fresh water. Later, after their children killed Apsu, she became the monstrous embodiment of primordial chaos, creating many dragons and demons. Tiamat was killed by the storm-god Marduk. The heavens and the earth were formed from her divided body.

17. Egyptian — **Apep (Apophis)** — In ancient Egyptian religion, Apep was a large golden snake and the enemy of Ra, the sun god. Apep lurked just before dawn, in the so-called Tenth Region of the Night, waiting to attack Ra (the sun) when he came across the horizon. Solar eclipses were caused by Apep when he succeeded in defeating Ra.

18. Tatar — **Zilant** — A legendary creature that has been the official symbol of the Russian city of Kazan since a 1730 royal decree, Zilant was described in the edict as a "black snake, crowned with the gold crown of Kazan, red-winged on the white field." Zilant is a part of Tatar and Russian folklore and is mentioned in legends about the origin of Kazan.

19. Russian — **Zmey Gorynych** — In Russia and the Ukraine, Zmey Gorynych was a fat, green, three-headed dragon who walked on two back paws, had small front paws, and spat fire. As a rule, Russian dragons usually have heads in multiples of three. Some have heads that grow back if every single head isn't cut off at the same time. Zmey Gorynych was supposedly slain by the legendary hero Dobrynya Nikitich.

20. Armenian — **Vishap** — Armenian dragons were said to live on Mt. Ararat, beneath lakes or in the clouds. Their blood was said to be so poisonous that any weapon dipped in it would kill instantly. Unlike most dragons in Western mythology, the Vishaps had long flowing hair and would sometimes transform into the form of three sisters. Vishap stones (giant stone markers) may have been created in their honor. Legends of these dragons prevailed even into Christian times.

21. Polish — **Wawel Dragon** — Also known as the Dragon of Wawel Hill, the Wawel Dragon is a famous dragon in Polish folklore. His lair was in a cave at the foot of Wawel Hill on the bank of the Vistula River in Krakow. Wawel Cathedral and Wawel Castle now stand on Wawel Hill. The cathedral features a statue of the Wawel dragon and a plaque commemorating his defeat by the Polish prince Krakus, who, according to legend, founded the city and his palace over the slain dragon's den. The dragon's cave below the castle is now a popular tourist attraction.

22. English — **Wyvern** — A legendary winged creature with a dragon's head, reptilian body, two legs, and a barbed tail, a wyvern is said to breathe fire or possess a venomous bite. Wyverns have been depicted in heraldry on shields, coats of arms, and banners for hundreds of years, and are a symbol of strength and endurance. They appear in medieval and modern European and British literature as well as a multitude of video and tabletop roleplaying games.

23. English — **Lindworm** — Although officially the word Lindworm refers to a wingless dragon with two legs and a venomous bite, it is often used in myth to refer to any serpentine dragon. A Lindworm was said to eat cattle and other livestock whole. It would also invade churches and churchyards and eat the dead from their graves. To keep this monster at bay, cattle would be offered as a sacrifice — no less than one animal per day just to keep it satisfied.

24. Anglo-Saxon — **Beowulf Dragon** — In the final act of the medieval Anglo-Saxon poem *Beowulf,* the hero fights a dragon, the third monster he encounters in the epic. The Beowulf dragon was one of the first fire-breathing dragons in western literature, and the inspiration for Smaug in J. R. R. Tolkien's *The Hobbit.*

25. Welsh — **Y Ddraig Goch** — The Red Dragon appears on the national flag of Wales. It is a mark of bravery and victory, and has been the symbol for the Welsh people since the Middle Ages. In Arthurian legend, the appearance of the Red Dragon is seen as a prophecy for the coming of King Arthur.

26. Norse — **Fafnir** — In the late 13th century *Volsunga Saga* of Iceland, Fáfnir was a young dwarf prince. He guarded his father's house of glittering gold and gems. He became very ill-natured and greedy, eventually turning into dragon (often a symbol of greed) to guard his treasure. Fáfnir then breathed poison into the air around him so that no one would go near him and his treasure. He was later slain by the young hero Sigurd.

27. Norse — **Nidhogg** — In Norse mythology Nidhogg is a monstrous dragon that gnaws at the roots of Yggdrasil, the World Tree, threatening to destroy it. Nidhogg uses the squirrel Ratatoskr to deliver messages to and from the eagle that perches on the top of Yggdrasil.

28. French — **Tarasque** — A legendary dragon from southern France, the Tarasque had six legs and a body covered with a turtle-like shell. After devastating the countryside, the Tarasque was attacked by the King's armies, but they could not defeat it. Finally, Saint Martha found the dragon and was able to charm it with hymns and prayers. She led the tamed beast back to the city, but the terrified people attacked it and killed it.

29. Christian — **St. George and the Dragon** — According to the *Golden Legend,* a medieval collection of stories on the lives of saints, the city of Silene was plagued by a monstrous dragon. To appease the dragon, the people of Silene fed it two sheep every day, and when the sheep failed, they fed it their children, chosen by lottery. Saint George defeated the dragon and helped convert the townsfolk to Christianity.

30. Incan — **Amaru** — Featuring a llama's head, a fox's mouth, the wings of a condor, the body of a snake, and a fish tail, the Amaru was a legendary dragon of Incan mythology. It was said to have been born from the tears of the god Waitapallana and it saved the people of Peru from a devastating drought.